What Next, Baby Bear!

Jill Murphy

A Puffin Pied Piper

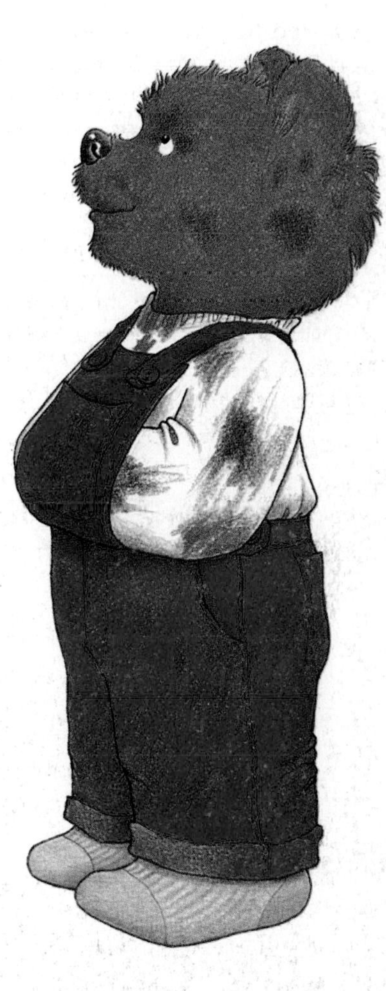

First published in the United States 1984 by
Dial Books for Young Readers
A Division of Penguin Books USA Inc.
375 Hudson Street
New York, New York 10014

Published in Great Britain by
Macmillan Publishers Ltd.

Library of Congress Catalog Card Number: 83-7316
Printed in Hong Kong by South China Printing Co.
First Pied Piper Printing 1986
US
10 9 8 7

WHAT NEXT, BABY BEAR!
is published in a hardcover edition by
Dial Books for Young Readers.
ISBN 0-14-054982-X

“Can I go to the moon?” asked Baby Bear.

“No, you can’t,” said Mrs. Bear.
“It’s bathtime.
Anyway, you’d have to find a rocket first.”

Baby Bear found a rocket
in the closet under the stairs.

He found a space helmet
on the drainboard in the kitchen
and a pair of space boots on the
mat by the front door.

He packed his teddy bear
and some food for the journey,
and took off up the chimney. . . .

FRAGILE

WHOOSH! Out into the night.

FRAGILE

An owl flew past.
"What a great rocket," he said.
"Where are you going?"
"To the moon," said Baby Bear.
"Would you like to come too?"
"Yes, please," said the owl.

An airplane roared out of the clouds.
Baby Bear waved and
some of the passengers waved back.

On and on they flew,
up and up, above the clouds,
past millions of stars, until
at last they landed on the moon.

FRAGILE

“There’s nobody here,” said Baby Bear.
“There are no trees,” said the owl.
“It’s kind of boring,” said Baby Bear.
“Should we have a picnic?”
“What a good idea!” said the owl.

"We'd better go," said Baby Bear.
"My bath must be ready by now."
Off they went, down and down.
The owl got out and flew away.
"Good-bye," he said. "It was nice
to meet you."

It rained and
the rain dripped through
Baby Bear's helmet.

Home went Baby Bear—
back down the chimney
and onto the living room carpet
with a BUMP!

FRAGILE

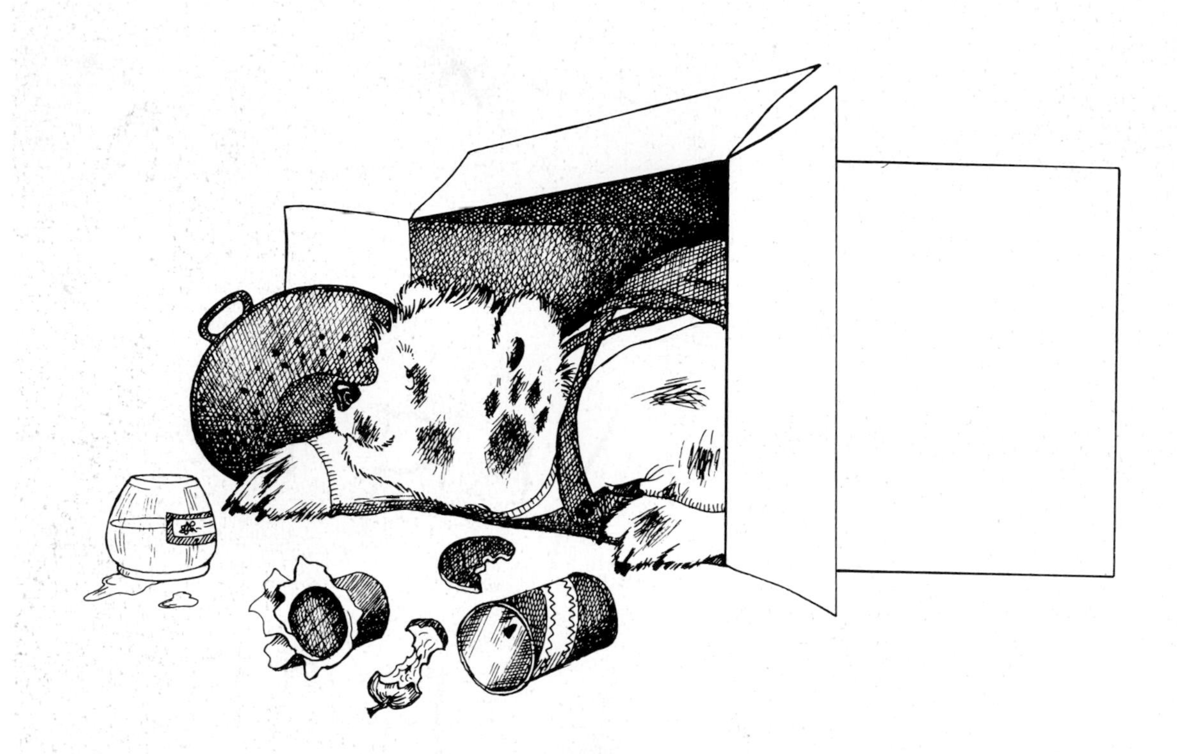

Mrs. Bear came into the room.
"How did you get so dirty?" she gasped,
as she took him to the bathroom.
"You look like you've been up the chimney."

"I *have*!" said Baby Bear.
"First, I found a rocket.
Then I put on my space helmet.
And then I flew to the moon."
"Oh, my," said Mrs. Bear, laughing.
"What will you think of next!"